LITVOICE N

AN INTERNATIONAL MONTHLY MAGAZINE

LITVOICE

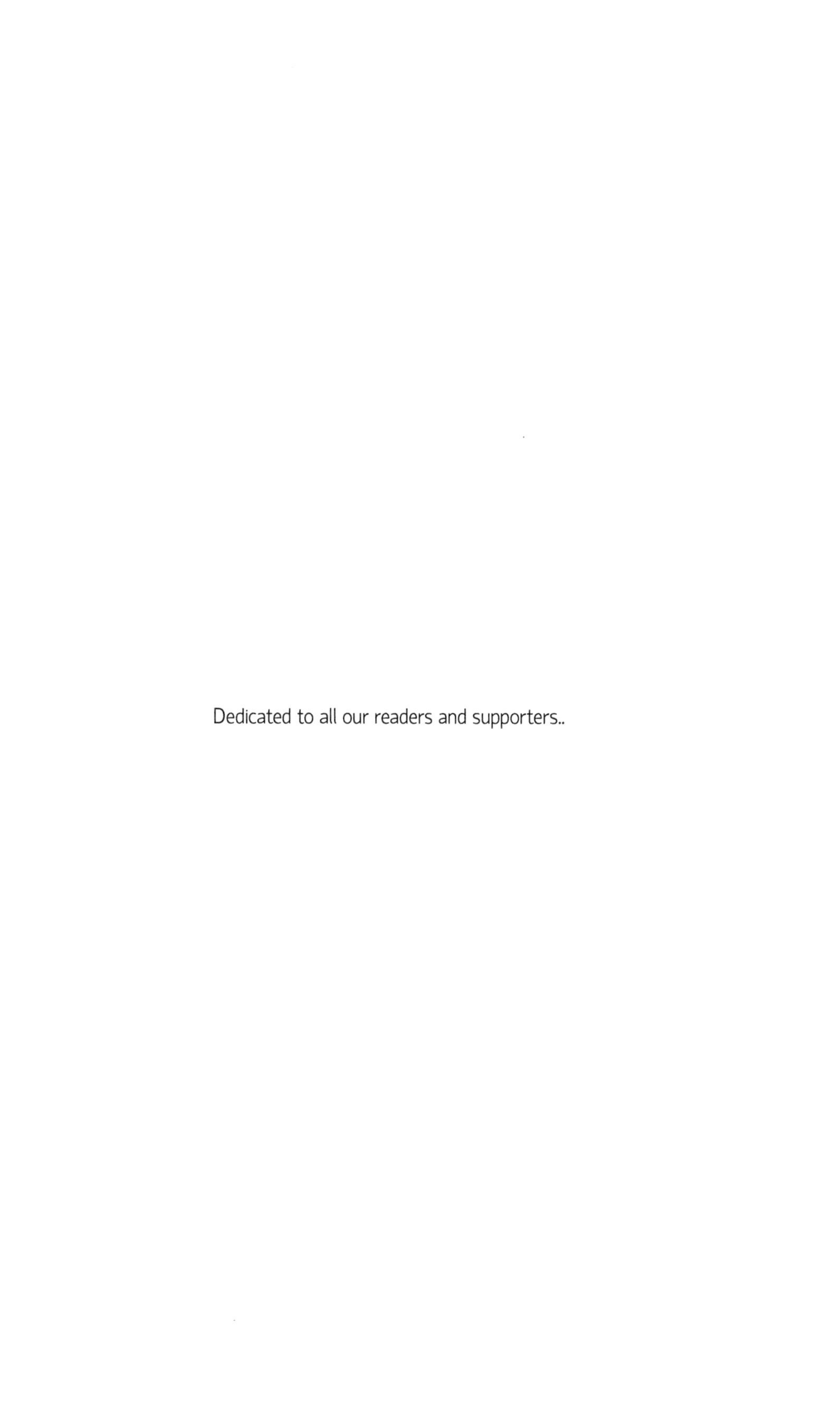

Dedicated to all our readers and supporters..

Contents

Foreword

" Literary voice " is a magazine of young writers. To express and to showcase their talent across the world.

Our own personal grouse with linguistic writing is that a great deal of it is far too technical for

(1) A general reader and

(2) A reader who doesn't want to fall asleep.

This is symptomatic of academic writing as a whole, of course; but that implies just how much of linguistics remains difficult to access if you don't have the requisite training and vocabulary (whose required level of familiarity sometimes boggles the mind).

I think a lot of what happens in linguistics is really, really good work that deserves to be recognized and championed for its worth and value to society, and used in multidisciplinary attempts to make the world a better place. Unfortunately, a lot of it can't reach the non-academically inclined person with big ideas because it's difficult to read and make sense of.

Preface

This is our 57th issue of " LitVoice " to reveal the voice of our unrevealed writers and poets...you can submit your writing on our instgram handle @litVoice and get published.

Our aim is to showcase their unrevaled talent.... It's a passion. A love of words, and sentences, and subjectivities that make us all very much imperfect, and very much human, as we struggle to find words to express what we think and feel.

It remains only for me to thank you, my dear, cherished, highly sought-after reader. Thank you for reading this and supporting us, and I hope you come to love language as much as we do.

Welcome to "LitVoicc". Let's reveal the world together...

With love.

Editor-in-Chief

Ms. Agarta Shanaya Shukla

Acknowledgements

LitVoice . We are Revealing Magazine for all ..now you all must think why this Name .. but " Literary Voice" was a better fit: it collocates nicely with a strong impact, this magazine is just an idea for giving us English Language majors something to do in our spare time. [There's another, even better reason, but I'll let you, the keen-eyed reader, figure it out].....hurray ..lets begin ...

CHAPTER ONE

Cover story –Lamiya Siraj – The Literary Luminary of Abu Dhabi

Lamiya Siraj

Lamiya Siraj, a versatile writer and celebrated author, proudly calls Abu Dhabi, U.A.E., her home. She is the brilliant mind behind captivating novels such as "Destined to Heal Within," "Desire or Guilt," and "Hidden Quest," along with the compelling non-fiction book "One Step Ahead." Lamiya's life journey, as diverse as her literary works, has seen her traverse multiple roles, reflecting her wide-ranging interests and experiences.

A Journey Through Words and Worlds

Lamiya Siraj's professional history is as varied as her bibliography. From an ex-banker at ICICI and Standard Chartered in India to a dedicated writer in Abu Dhabi, her path has been one of constant evolution. Relocating to Abu Dhabi in 2006 to support her husband, Lamiya discovered her true calling in writing, which led her to become a renowned author, blogger, and columnist. Her initial foray into writing began with an article in Friday Magazine's Viewpoint section in 2018, which paved the way for her prolific career. Since then, her thought-provoking pieces have appeared in major newspapers and online platforms across the U.A.E., India, and beyond. ### Life as an Author Lamiya's journey as an author is a testament to self-discovery and perseverance. Initially, she penned her thoughts in a private journal, never intending to share them with the world. However, during a period of forced rest following surgery in her mid-thirties, she began writing for a magazine. The unexpected publication of her anecdote, coupled with praise from family and friends, revealed her hidden talent. Despite early rejections, Lamiya learned to write authentically, allowing her creativity to flourish. Her determination led her to craft short stories and eventually, novels. Today, she proudly boasts three novels and a non-fiction book, with each work resonating deeply with readers. ### Literary Accomplishments Lamiya's first book, "One Step Ahead," released in 2019, showcases her knack for transforming real-life experiences into engaging narratives. Her debut novel, "Destined to Heal Within," released in 2021, received critical acclaim and prestigious awards, including The Firefoxx Award for Best Fiction Writer and the Best Writer award from NE8x. "Desire or Guilt" and "Hidden Quest" further solidify her reputation, with each novel weaving intricate tales of personal growth, love, and adventure.

Beyond the Written World

Lamiya's passions extend beyond writing. She is an avid reader, traveler, photographer, and sports enthusiast. Her keen observations of the world around her enrich her storytelling, bringing authenticity and depth to her characters and narratives. Despite her busy schedule, Lamiya finds joy in spending time with her daughter, nurturing a cherished mother-daughter bond that underscores the many facets of her life.

Recognition and Impact

Lamiya Siraj's contributions to literature have not gone unnoticed. She has received numerous accolades, including the Title of "Best Author of The Year 2023" from INKZOID FOUNDATION and multiple awards from NE8x, Fanatixx-Spectrum, AwardsArc, Firefoxx, and Applause. Her articles, short stories, and contributions to various anthologies have garnered praise from readers, bloggers, social media communities, event organizers, and publishers alike. Lamiya's story is a powerful reminder of the transformative power of passion and perseverance. Her journey from banking to writing, marked by challenges and triumphs, inspires aspiring writers and readers around the world. As she continues to pen her narratives, Lamiya Siraj remains a beacon of creativity and resilience in the literary world.

CHAPTER TWO

Say No to Violence

The International Day of Non-Violence is observed on 2 October, the birthday of Mahatma Gandhi, leader of the Indian independence movement and pioneer of the philosophy and strategy of non-violence.

According to General Assembly resolution A/RES/61/271 of 15 June 2007, which established the commemoration, the International Day is an occasion to "disseminate the message of non-violence, including through education and public awareness". The resolution reaffirms "the universal relevance of the principle of non-violence" and the desire "to secure a culture of peace, tolerance, understanding and non-violence".

Introducing the resolution in the General Assembly on behalf of 140 co-sponsors, India's Minister of State for External Affairs, Mr. Anand Sharma, said that the wide and diverse sponsorship of the resolution was a reflection of the universal respect for Mahatma Gandhi and of the enduring relevance of his philosophy. Quoting the late leader's own words, he said: "Non-violence is the greatest force at the disposal of mankind. It is mightier than the mightiest weapon of destruction devised by the ingenuity of man".

Background

The life and leadership of Mahatma Gandhi

Gandhi, who helped lead India to independence, has been the inspiration for non-violent movements for civil rights and social change across the world. Throughout his life, Gandhi remained committed to his belief in non-violence even under oppressive conditions and in the face of seemingly insurmountable challenges.

The theory behind his actions, which included encouraging massive civil disobedience to British law as with the historic Salt March of 1930, was that "just means lead to just ends"; that is, it is irrational to try to use violence to achieve a peaceful society. He believed that Indians must not use violence or hatred in their fight for freedom from colonialism.

Definition of Non-Violence

The principle of non-violence — also known as non-violent resistance — rejects the use of physical violence in order to achieve social or political change. Often described as "the politics of ordinary people", this form of social struggle has been adopted by mass populations all over the world in campaigns for social justice.

Professor Gene Sharp, a leading scholar on non-violent resistance, uses the following definition in his publication, The Politics of Nonviolent Action:

"Nonviolent action is a technique by which people who reject passivity and submission, and who see struggle as essential, can wage their conflict without violence. Nonviolent action is not an attempt to avoid or ignore conflict. It is one response to the problem of how to act effectively in politics, especially how to wield powers effectively."

While non-violence is frequently used as a synonym for pacifism, since the mid-twentieth century the term non-violence has been adopted by many movements for social change which do not focus on opposition to war.

One key tenet of the theory of non-violence is that the power of rulers depends on the consent of the population, and non-violence therefore seeks to undermine such power through withdrawal of the consent and cooperation of the populace.

There are three main categories of non-violence action: protest and persuasion, including marches and vigils; non-cooperation; and non-violent intervention, such as blockades and occupations.

CHAPTER THREE

10 Books you should read to get rid of summer blues

1. Sarah Perry, Melmoth
(Custom House)

I hate horror movies (yes, I'm a scaredy cat) but I love books that fall into the surreal/eerie/uncanny category, which I think is what I'll find in Melmoth. Sarah Perry's new novel follows a translator with a mysterious past. She's afraid it's caught up to her when, one day, a friend shows up with a strange manuscript, detailing all sorts of horror stories, each involving a shadowy figure that lurks in obscure folklore, known as Melmoth. Since Halloween is almost upon us, I'm particularly excited to delve into this spooky story of magic and mythology.

–Katie Yee, LitVoice assistant writer.

2. Lou Berney, November Road
(William Morrow)

November Road is the new book that everyone in the crime and mystery world seems to be talking about. And with good reason. Berney's story starts with the JFK assassination and morphs into a relentlessly moving (and relentlessly engaging) fugitive story, as two figures on the run find their lives intersected and set toward a common fate. Berney's voice is strong and human and his characters have rich emotional lives of their own. There's an incredible momentum to the story, a true thriller punctuated with moments of brilliant humanity.

–Dwyer Murphy, CrimeReads senior editor

3.Annick Smith and Susan O'Connor, Hearth: A Global Conversation on Identity, Community, and Place
(Milkweed Editions)

My wife and I are expecting a child in January, so we've been talking a lot lately about family, home, and the kind of place we hope to create for a child born into our perpetually troubled world. Hearth: A Global Conversation on Identity, Community, and Place, has arrived at a fortuitous time for us. A wide-ranging anthology devoted to the idea and symbol of the hearth, a traditional centerpiece of the home, the collection avoids nostalgia and deals squarely with how community and place can be approached and enacted in a world torn by immigration crises, climate change, and inequality.

–Stephen Sparks, LitVoice contributing editor

4. Tana French, The Witch Elm

(Viking)

In recent months, I've been reading a lot of experimental and surrealist literary fiction, which I love—but I have to admit I've worn myself down a bit. This week, I started in on Tana French's latest novel, The Witch Elm, and it is absolutely thrilling in its regular novel-ness. This is not to say it's boring—not in the least. It's just a real, regular, 500-page novel, with lush, detailed descriptions, large family trees, actual scenes, nagging mysteries, and prose so smooth you forget about it and just sink right in. I doubt that, at page 150, I even have any real idea what this book is going to be, but so far it's exactly what I need right now.

–Emily Temple, LitVoice senior editor

5. Claire Fuller, Bitter Orange

(Tin House Books)

I love a protagonist who's lonely and socially uncertain, particularly when she's forced into proximity to the people whose lives she desires (see also: Prep), so I'm very excited to read Claire Fuller's Bitter Orange. According to Alex Clark at The Guardian, its thoughtful loner, Frances, is also an unreliable narrator (even better!), and Fuller's "talent for the sinister" pervades the story of her relationship with the glamorous-seeming couple who she meets at a ramshackle country house. A beguiled introvert, a manor in disrepair, and other people's secrets? Easy sell.

–Jessie Gaynor, LitVoice social media editor

6. Joe Ide, Wrecked

(Mulholland Books)

Joe Ide first entered onto the mystery scene two years ago with IQ, his first crime novel, and the first in a series to feature genius investigator Isaiah Quintabe (known as IQ to his few friends and many clients), solving crimes in South Central LA. Wrecked, Ide's third in the series, is sure to please fans with its mixture of unique setting, complex action sequences, and frequent nods to Sherlockian inspirations. In Wrecked, IQ and his former partner-in-crime Dodson are now official partners in investigations, and trying to make their business a tad more professional while also looking into a missing persons case. I can't wait to finish this caper-style comedy – Ide obeys the rule of Chekov's gun, and his books always end in a glorious mixture of chaos, violence, and and an impeccably choreographed shoot out.

–**Molly Odintz,**

7. Susan Orlean, The Library Book
(Simon & Schuster)

Orlean's new book, which looks at the 1986 blaze that destroyed 400,000 books and damaged 700,000 more in the Los Angeles Public Library, is the unsolved mystery coupled with a love letter to libraries that I didn't know I needed!

–**Emily Firetog, LitVoice managing editor**

8. Sarah Stone, Hungry Ghost Theater
(WTAW Press)

Sarah Stone's Hungry Ghost Theater is an astonishing mosaic of fiction, theater, lyrical text and performance, tracing one family through many generations and permutations. It's a rare look at the inner workings of a theater company devoted to political material, involving siblings Robert and Julia, as well as an exploration of the roots of empathy, undertaken by their sister Eva, a neuroscientist. Reading it leaves the aftertaste of a powerful performance: "Though we'd worked all summer for one ephemeral moment, I was content."

–**Jane Ciabattari, LitVoice columnist**

9. Seth Fletcher, Einstein's Shadow: A Black Hole, a Band of Astronomers, and the Quest to See the Unseeable
(Ecco)

For as long as humans have existed we've gazed up at the night sky in wonder. In the last 100 years, technological and scientific breakthroughs have allowed us to look even farther, up to millions, even billions, of lightyears into space. But for all our achievements, no one has been able to capture a photo of one of the universe's most mysterious phenomena—a black hole. Shep Doeleman , a Harvard astronomer, is very close, however, and his plan to get the capture is chronicled in Seth Fletcher's fascinating book Einstein's Shadow: A Black Hole, a Band of Astronomers, and the

Quest to See the Unseeable. Fletcher follows Doeleman and his team of international scientists for five years as they work to assemble the equipment necessary to take the photo. Their story is rife with exciting breakthroughs and heartbreaking disappointments. If you're a space nerd like me, this book is not to be missed.

–Amy Brady, LitVoice contributor

10. Jeff Jackson, Destroy All Monsters (FSG Originals)

Whether he's writing about haunted subcultures or the end of the world, Jeff Jackson has a way of balancing surreal settings with painfully realistic group dynamics. His new novel Destroy All Monsters looks poised to continue that, telling the story of an epidemic of murders of musicians, told through two complimentary narratives. Structurally bold and thematically resonant, this is a welcome addition to Jackson's bibliography.

–Tobias Carroll, LitVoice contributor

CHAPTER FOUR

Authors Interview – Steffy Terrance

Author Steffy Terrance

Q1. Tell us a bit about yourself.
Hi, I am Steffy Terrance, a 20-year old student. The author of 'The Rhythm to Soar'.

Q2. How did publishing your first book change your process of writing?
I believe the writing process has become more open and honest to the audience. The primary basis of what I write is honesty, to depict all of the

emotions in the right manner.

Q3. If you could tell your younger writing self, anything, and what would it be?
I would say trust in yourself and trust the process. I remember the time when I first started writing. It wasn't perfect. I was just eleven then back in school.

Q4. What does literary success look like to you?
I personally don't believe success can be defined by any sort of materialistic things. In the book, The Rhythm to soar, there are poems which tell pain, hope and solitude. If the readers are able to resonate with the poems and the message conveyed, I feel that's real success and happiness.

Q5. Does your family support your career as a writer?
Yes, my family and friends has been a great support for me during this process. And I am very thankful to each one of them.

Q6. What one thing would you give up to become a better writer?
I think to portray any character or story in the right way, will be to let go of the inhibitions. I think I have been better at letting go of certain inhibitions and to tell stories which are raw and honest.

Q7. Who's your Inspiration in the literary field?
I feel like each writer has a different way of depicting stories, or emotions. I have liked the books of Paulo Coelho and Vikram seth. Classics by Sarojini Naidu have inspired me a lot.

Q8. What kind of research do you do, and how long do you spend researching
before beginning a book?
For me the most of the work is after I finish the book. Mostly to check if all of the thoughts and emotions are conveyed in the right manner, also regarding editorial section. Before the book I just let these emotions flow so I think it doesn't take
much time.

Q9. What's the turning point of your life when you realize you want to be an

author?

I have always wanted to be a writer. Like I said earlier I wrote my first poem when I was eleven. I have always been curious about books and stories.

Q10. How long on average does it take you to write a book?

I haven't thought of it like that. Mainly because I don't work within a specific time period. Writing is a natural process to me. So, I would just pen each emotions and thoughts as it flows.

Q11. What are your favorite literary books?

There are a lot actually. The alchemist by Paulo Coelho, Ancient promises by Jayshree misra, The Go between by L.P.Hartley and the list goes on.

Q12. Why have you selected to write in this genre?

I have loved poetry my entire life. To me, poetry is like a song with a soul. It has a rhythm within it. It is like a beat. And poetry can convey the emotions appropriately.

Q13. Do you hide any secrets in your books that only a few people will find? There are some poems which need a strong intellect to understand the meanings.

But most of the other ones are purely heart-touching. I don't think there aren't

any secrets as such but the poem I want people to know will be 'The voices at

tussle to Guard' dedicated to the health care workers as all of us are fighting the

pandemic together.

Q14. Do you view writing as a kind of spiritual practice?

More than spiritual practice, I think, it has been a process for me to liberate certain emotions and feelings.

Q15. What's the best way to market your books?

I think the best way to market any book is to make it known to the particular group of people the story has higher chance to resonate with. Although, there are

readers choosing all genres, people who like poetry more tend to read it more.

Yes, social media marketing is also one of the strategies which is very easy and

convenient.

CHAPTER FIVE

Open letter to brother - A Blessed sister

Dear bro,

The most anticipated day of the year have come again but the tragedy of this day is that, unlike all the years that we have spent this day together, this year we are so far apart. It feels off-kilter and sad all at the same time. I wish we had been together this Rakhi as well, doing all our conventional leg pulling and teasing the way we used to.

I am blessed to have a brother like you and the words won't justify the amount of respect and love I have for you. As mother fondly recalls the time when I first arrived, you were scared to hold me, you were scared that this miniature baby would crumble if you touch her so much and I may somehow vanish. You were fascinated by my small hands and spend counting each finger twice a day. A four-year-old boy got a little toy to play with and he was ecstatic. This baby grew up to be your partner-in-crime, playmate, little nuisance and sometimes a total pain in the ass.

You made me what I am today. You made me strong, wild, independent and sassy. We have made the plethora of memories together and played countless of made up games throughout the day and night. If I never had your calming presence, I would have been a sad case of a classic spoilt brat but you grounded me.

We shared our own secret world of imaginary pirates, you were Peter Pan and I was one of the lost boys, fighting captain Hook, climbing imaginary mountains, going on epic quests for lost treasures. It was just you, me and our backyard. How can I forget all the senseless things we tried and got trashed within the inch of our life?

This day all the memories are replaying through my brain on an endless loop. I wish I can somehow transcend space and time and reach you to tie that one sacred thread and not break the one ritual that we have been doing together since we were in diapers. As a kid, we did this to satisfy our mother and competed over who has better rakhi. I was jealous of the shiny diamonds and pretty designs that winked at me from your wrist. So, I would cry and you would always remove the shiniest rakhi from your wrist and tie it on mine. As we grew older, it was not a competition anymore but a deep sense of sentimentality and emotions whenever I tied it on your wrist. It was renewal of the promise that we shared and a ritual that promised so much without uttering a single word. I will terribly miss this ritual because it signifies that we have been through so much. We have grown up together with our grandmother's stories whispering magical realms into our ears, weaving dream worlds distant and untouched and the echoes of gods mighty and strong. It shows that we have shared bruises, tears and all the mighty adventures that makes the childhood most beautiful phase ever.

So, even though we are far apart, our heart is still together. It lies in the distant fields of unripe maize where we played hide and seek, it still beats in the silent echoes of the laughter that we shared while rolling down the hills and it would always find it's peace at the end of the day in the childish antics buried deep in our memories. Photographs can only capture frozen memories but this heart replays those memories and brings it to life. I'll always cherish these memories in my heart. Forever.

Yours Lovingly,
A Sister that still trails behind you

CHAPTER SIX

Abhay's Suicide Note – Shagnick Bhattacharya

There was a knock on the door. It was the sweeper, like every morning after breakfast. I was still half-asleep, lying in my bed. Subhash, my roommate, opened the door. While I had missed my breakfast today, he had woken up at the same time he gets up everyday, had his breakfast and was now studying at his table,

before he went up to answer the door. In came the sweeper with his broom and a register, and handed the latter, with a pen in it, to Subhash. It was the room cleaning record register, and my roommate

put his signature against today's date, acknowledging the cleaning of the room. This was a boy's hostel where we stayed, in Kirby Place, near the Base Hospital, in Delhi. It was the temporary residence of about a hundred college students of Delhi University. I and Subhash were living in room number 4 of this hostel

together for about a year. Both of us were in the same college in the University – Delhi College of Arts and Commerce. He is in first year History honours, while I am a fresher student of B.Com program. Both of us are Bengalis - he from Calcutta, and I from Barrackpore. Needless to say, we are quite good friends.

The sweeper was done with our room. I requested him to do the bathroom as well.

Subhash Roy aspires to be an Archaeologist. He is a tall, fair, spectacled guy, not very good-looking I might add, a little overweight too. But such ingenuity as he possesses is rarely found in other people of his age. He does not talk to everyone in the hostel out of a notion of superiority, but is well-respected by everyone here owing to his disciplined life, helpful behaviour towards anyone who needs help, as well as a good sense of humour. Oh yes, and I am Bhaskar Chatterjee, of the same height and complexion as his, just physically much more fit than him. I want to become an author, and that is a major reason why I am now writing about my thrilling experience of that day. If you, as my reader, don't believe this account, then I cannot blame you. That human existence is so very transient and that insignificance can still be so

significant is something that I – and most of the people – wouldn't have understood before.

After the sweeper left the room after cleaning, Subhash sat on his chair, and continued studying after saying casually, "Probably Abhay didn't wake up today". When I asked why, he didn't reply.

Every hostel has at least one overly introvert guy. Abhay Gaur was the one in our hostel, a meticulous and neat fellow. Second year, Chemistry honours. He and his roommate, Aniket Mishra, lived in the neighbouring room number 3. Seeing him studying seriously, I did not insist on an answer and went to the bathroom for a bath. After all, it's not everyday that you get to use the bathroom immediately

after it has been cleaned afresh. My eyes for once just glanced at the clock on the wall – it was around exactly 9 AM.

Abhay's suicide note ran thus: "I just cannot take it anymore. My life is nothing but eternal suffering. I guess everyone's life is like that, but I don't chose to spend my precious life like this. My name, Abhay, means fearless. And fearless I shall be. There is no shame in the step I'm about to take. I feel proud that I have the power to do what I'm about to. Not everyone can do this. Especially alone, without any help. But it's a different matter that I don't need any help in doing what I must do. I know my parents will feel bad when the world gets to know. I am their only son after all. Even I feel bad. I was leading such a good life. I had so many dreams. If only things wouldn't have gone so wrong lately.... I have no other choice now. I'm ashamed of my past. But I won't let my past dominate my future. This is the only way that I can save my as well as my family's honour."

I will attempt to give a little description here. The dead body was found sitting on the chair, with a verical cut mark across his artery on the left arm. The blade with which it was done, was in his right arm, grasped rather lightly. His face resembled that of a man sleeping peacefully. His dark skin was unchanged, and his head leaned upon his chest. Both his arms were placed on the table, under which was the suicide note. The note was a page torn out of his diary, which was nearby on his bed. The handwriting was no doubt his.

Aniket had gone out of the hostel at 9:10 AM that day to attend classes in his college. We discovered the body at around 2 PM, when Subhash observed that Abhay, a man who so strictly followed his routine, did not show up even for lunch at the hostel mess. Subhash, I and a few others had then went to check on his

room. The door was closed, but not locked. Indrajit, Abhay's closest friend in the hostel, went in first. He could not believe what he was seeing. At first, he thought his friend was pranking him by sitting in such an eerie manner. I took Indrajit to my room, and tried to comfort him. He was crying – something hard to imagine on his tough face. After taking a good look (with a surpringly stern and emotionless

face), Subhash called in the police, then informed the hostel warden. The police came in about half an hour later. Abhay's body was sent for autopsy in the nearby Base hospital. Preliminary report would arrive in a day. The final report would take much longer. Aniket came back from college a little after 3 PM.

When he was informed about what had happened, he sadly, but calmly, admitted that Abhay was behaving a little depressed lately. He regretted that he could not make out that Abhay would have committed suicide. Indeed, Abhay was a kind of guy all of us knew to be someone who did not need anyone's help in anything. It was what he himself believed about himself. The officer-in-charge asked us a few very simple questions from us all who knew him. The police could not find any meaningful reason for the suicide. The best reason we could find is his consistent poor academic performance, and a breakup to a year-long relationship about a week ago. At last, the parents of the deceased were informed. I cannot imagine how they must have felt. All I know is that they rushed from Patna for Delhi at once, for I heard that by midnight they had seen the corpse, and began preparations for Abhay's last rites.

Life in a hostel is supposed to be the best part of one's life. At least that's what my father had told me. Ironically, someone I knew had ended his life in this supposed-to-be paradise. The entire hostel was sad.

Subhash had been acting very strange ever since the body was discovered. He was not talking to almost anyone in the hostel (I being the notable exception), and carried a constant grim expression on his face. It was hard to believe then that he might be traumatised too. Probably just out of the need for a little fresh air, he went out of the hostel for a stroll today morning for about an hour after breakfast, around 7:40 AM. But that was not the case – he was not traumatised at all. He was after something, as I got to know later.

At 10 AM, Subhash texted me: "Come quickly to the common room with as many people as possible". I was confused. And nervous too of what was going to happen, but I obeyed. The common room of our hostel was a quite small room, a cross breed of a library and an indoor games room. I could bring only about 10 people with me, including Aniket and Indrajit. Subhash was sitting alone in a corner when we entered,

thinking about something. As we entered, he stood up. "I have an announcement to make here right now," he said. "Make yourselves comfortable, and then we shall begin." When everyone was settled across the room, each one sitting in a chair turned towards the centre where he stood, Subhash began.

"Suicide," he said grimly, "is not just someone taking his own life. It is the culmination of a long process. This aspect of suicide is very less understood..." Two of the hostelites, who were going past the room at the moment, entered the room on seeing so many people assembled without the warden nearby.

"...It is true that Abhay was becoming increasingly irregular towards his end. But no one suspected that he would take his own life. The truth is, he did not. He was murdered." Absolute silence. No one could believe what they were hearing. And who they were hearing it from.

"We tend to think of suicide as an easy way out of the miseries of life. What we miss out is the fact that it takes courage. Slitting one's own wrist with a blade is not an easy thing to do. It involves the giving up of all attachments from life. Yet evidence points to Abhay's being able to do it in the first attempt, as well as

without any apparent reason for suicide. Interestingly, I observed that the entire suicide note did not contain even a single reference to words like suicide and death. It is a very poor suicide note, if it is one, which does not clearly state the reason, or who is to blame, or who is not to be. Thus Abhay's suicide note is a very bad one, or not a suicide note at all. Given the perfectionist that he was, the

former seems to be more improbable than the latter."

"So what was it then?", said Taranath, a senior of ours.

"A diary entry. The page was torn out of his diary, as we know. He had written it as a diary entry. It was his murderer who tore the page and placed it accordingly to create the illusion of a suicide note." Subhash's answer, however, still had a huge flaw.

"Abhay had clearly committed suicide. Are you saying that he wrote a diary entry, and then someone slit his wrist and fabricate a suicide?" I went on, "Even so, this method of suicide takes a certain amount of time to die, until he would have bled out to death. Are you suggesting that he just cooperated with his murderer?" "Not at all. And I am coming to that." Subhash said, "About an hour ago, I had a conversation with Mahesh. Ah yes, I'll take it that most of us here don't know his name – he is the sweeper guy. He had come to my room at his usual time for cleaning. You were in Indrajit's room then," he said, looking at me. " I asked him about what he had saw yesterday in Abhay's room while cleaning it. Apparently

many people have asked him the same, but no one figured out what was wrong. "What he said put in the last piece of the puzzle in place. He said that the room was very usual in appearance. Aniket was sitting on the side of his bed, tying up his shoes. Abhay was on that same place as we found him, although not as the

way we found him. He was sitting on his chair, his hands on the table lying over a piece of paper, with his right hand holding a ball pen in a precise grip. Additionally, he was breathing very heavily. Mahesh bhaiya understood that Abhay was sad, and that it would have been better not to have talked to him in

such a situation. The room cleaning record register was therefore signed, quite unusually, by Aniket. This last thing was noticed by me when I signed the register myself yesterday, as my room is just the next one.

"Another thing that is of quite interest is the fact that his hands were grasping a ball pen. The 'suicide note', with its thick letters, was clearly written by a gel pen. Hence I prove my point about murder. Now we can come to the point of how the murder was executed. "Aniket, can you answer a question of mine?", Subhash looked towards Aniket, "I wonder what you know about rocuronium?"

Aniket replied, puzzled, "What is that ?" Subhash shrugged his shoulders, then explained. "Rocuronium is a steroid-based neuromuscular-blocking drug, usually used in general anaesthesia. It paralyses all the muscles in the body. It is my firm belief that somehow Abhay was made to ingest this drug. The usual route of administering this drug is intravenous, or from he veins, and it's swallowing in any way can cause a bunch of hazardous side effects on a living person, like vomiting, slurred speech or even coma. But Abhay was already dead before such effects could have taken place. "I would make a confession here. Today morning, after breakfast, I had gone to the hospital to offer my condolences to Abhay's parents, as well as to get an idea of the direction in which the autopsy was heading. It was by sheer luck, I must say, that I found out that a component of general anaesthesia was missing from a surgeon's stores there on the day before yesterday, when I overheard a conversation between two medical students. So the anaesthetic was stolen, directly or indirectly, by our murderer." Everyone's eyes were fixed on him. All but two minds in the entire room were confused.

"But let's get back to the topic. Once the drug would have got to work, Abhay would have become paralysed. Although he would have felt light headed, he could have roughly realised what was happening, but could do nothing. "The drug couldn't have been in his food, for all our meals are made in the hostel

mess. Therefore, it was in his water. Since just 0.6 mg of this drug is enough to induce a paralysis of at least 45 minutes, it would have left absolutely no trace on the now-empty water bottle. The murderer added the drug in the water bottle before Abhay would have got up in the morning. The drug would start working

within two minutes of Abhay's drinking water. Presumably Abhay was in the habit of drinking water after getting up or before having breakfast." Now Aniket asked the question which was in all our minds for the past few moments – "how are you jumping to this rocuronium bromide thing?" "I'm surprised how well you could pronounce the name of the drug in the first go, and also know it's full name," Subhash said. "As far as I know, none of the subjects you study in college has anything to do with general anaesthesia." Aniket looked angrily at Subhash. "Abhay committed suicide. You are overthinking too much now." His face had turned red.

"Rocuronium Bromide," replied Subhash, completely ignoring Aniket's last remark, "is known for increasing pulmonary vascular resistance. In simple words, it decreases the flow of blood from the heart to other parts of the body. When Abhay was under the effect of the anaesthetic, any cut on his body would have led to lower than usual loss of blood. "A little less important is the fact that while it is active, the drug has a particular side-effect on people who have asthma, like Abhay. Difficulty in breathing. This side-effect and Mahesh's account of Abhay's heavy breathing match perfectly. That is the importance of rocuronium in all this. I'll assume that the murderer had no idea about this side effect. "However, the ingenuity of this murderer lies in the fact of his play with timing. The post-mortem report would clearly put the time of death at around 9:35 AM. Which would put the time of Abhay's cutting his wrist in case of suicide between 9:20 AM and 9:25 AM, owing to the fact that death in this kind of suicide occurs within 10-15 minutes. The time of suicide thus indicated was when Abhay was alone in the room, since Aniket goes out of the hostel at 9:10 AM. For this, Aniket has two perfect alibis – the Security Guard who was on duty at the time at the main gate as well as the hostel check-out register. But owing to the thing about

pulmonary vascular resistance caused out of the anaesthetic, the actual cut could be inflicted just a little before 9:10 AM which would cause death around 9:35 -" Suddenly, Aniket got up from his chair and charged with all his might at Subhash. Subhash was prepared, but his physique was nothing compared to Aniket, who landed a punch on his face. Subhash fell. Aniket would have continued, but I andthe others quickly went and tightly grasped him. Knowing that it was over, Aniket didn't resist frantically for too long. "I'm calling the police," said Indrajit. He had finally regained his composure now. Subhash got up. "No," he said, "wait". He went up to where the boys were holding Aniket tightly. Aniket was giving him a very vicious stare. Subhash gave a nice blow of his fist on Aniket's head. Aniket grunted in pain, and then lost consciousness. "Now you may call the police," Subhash said. "And yes, someone inform the

warden too. This, my friends, is the murderer of Abhay Gaur." A long silence followed. I broke it after what seemed like an eternity, by asking Subhash, "how could this anaesthetic go undetectable in a post-mortem?"

Subhash looked at me with a smile. His nose was bleeding from the punch he had received from Aniket. His spectacles were miraculously intact. "Good observation", he said. Then he explained, "once rocuronium bromide's effect ends, the only minute traces of it left is found in the liver, which is in no way related to the slitting of one's artery in the wrist. These minute traces get even more insignificant by time, owing to its half-life of about one-and-a-half hours." "A question still remains," commented Subhash after some time, "that of the motive. It is not very clear, but I know what it is. Probably. Let the police interrogate him and find out for a certainty. They can do this job better than me." The police interrogation of Aniket Mishra led to us knowing of why he killed Abhay.

Both these men, Abhay and Aniket, were very talented students. But eventually they were misguided by some of their peers and got involved into petty politics of hooliganism. They were among a vast group of young people who were the pawns of morally corrupt politicians. They were assigned all kinds of jobs – arson, extortion, smuggling, beating people. However, Abhay was not made for such a life at all. The more he immersed in it, the more he felt the heavy weight of guilt on his shoulders. Over time, this started

taking a toll on him – his behaviour, his relationships, his academic potential – every aspect of his life. So, when his girlfriend dumped him, he realised that he was on a wrong path, and could not continue down it anymore. This thought of his became a conviction when he discovered just two days before his death that

they were being used as an instrument for instigating a major communal riot right here in Delhi. He just could not do it anymore. He told his roommate – who was one of the few friends he had – about his

decision to surrender to the police and tell them everything that he knows about the riots that would have taken place. Aniket found this change in Abhay's mind very surprising, and tried to talk him out of it. But Abhay was determined of his choice.

That night, Aniket went out in the evening for a jogging. He smuggled rocuronium bromide into the hostel in his own empty water bottle on his way back to hostel through the hospital complex. In this, he was helped by one of the janitors of the hospital.

The problem that day was created mainly because Abhay had woken up later than usual, as he was to go to the police station and not college. He woke up at 8:40 AM, and brushed his teeth, after which he drank a little water and then sat on his chair to see for once his yesterday's diary entry. It was then that the anaesthetic started its effect. So far, Aniket had just thought about perfectly fabricating a

suicide, but on seeing the open page of the diary before him, he had the idea of creating the illusion of a suicide note as well....

The police have taken due action. All the potential rioters have been arrested. Many rackets have been busted. As for Aniket, the District Court is to give its verdict on his fate tomorrow.

In a way, Subhash's intervention avoided a major communal riot. A nice way to begin our adventures together, I think.